Harriet Ziefert

41 Uses for a Cat

drawings by Todd McKie

Sterling Publishing Co., Inc.

New York

Published by Sterling Publishing Co., Inc.
387 Park Avenue South, New York, NY 10016

Text © 2004 by Harriet Ziefert
Illustrations © 2004 by Todd McKie

Distributed in Canada by Sterling Publishing
c/o Canadian Manda Group, One Atlantic Avenue, Suite 105
Toronto, Ontario, Canada M6K 3E7
Distributed in Great Britain by Chrysalis Books
64 Brewery Road, London N79NT, England
Distributed in Australia by Capricorn Link (Australia) Pty. Ltd.
P.O. Box 704, Windsor, NSW 2756, Australia

ISBN 1-4027-1616-8

Color separations by Bright Arts
Printed in China

10   9   8   7   6   5   4   3   2   1

For Judy
  —T.M.

1.

scarf

2.

bearer of gifts

3.

model

4.
backseat
driver

5.

floral arranger

6.

bird fancier

7.

mood elevator

8.

interior decorator

9.
massage therapist

10.
food critic

11.

hat

12.

confidante

13.
chair warmer

14.
psychiatrist

15.

surrogate child

16.
dog trainer

17.

keeper of secrets

18.
back scratcher

19.
significant other

20.
plate cleaner

21.
show-off

22.
Romeo

23.
athletic director

24.

doorman

25.

knitter's assistant

26.

gardener

27.

centerpiece

28.

messenger

29.

surgeon

30.
home improvement

31.

alarm clock

32.
acrobat

33.
hair brush

34.
ichthyologist

35.
lookout

36.
listener

37.

sous chef

38.
SPY

39.

crooner

40.
Flyswatter

41.

sculpture